The Reptile Club

To the boys of the École George–McDowell Reptile Club:
Alain, Marc, Paul, Kyle, Dan and Nick (Hiss, hiss!) — M.F.

For the most wonderful and adventurous little girl, Sabina Bailie — E.E.

Text © 2018 Maureen Fergus
Illustrations © 2018 Elina Ellis

Kids Can Press gratefully acknowledges the financial support of the Government of Ontario, through the Ontario Media Development Corporation; the Ontario Arts Council; the Canada Council for the Arts; and the Government of Canada, through the CBF, for our publishing activity.

Published in Canada and the U.S. by Kids Can Press Ltd.
25 Dockside Drive, Toronto, ON M5A 0B5

Kids Can Press is a Corus Entertainment Inc. company

www.kidscanpress.com

The artwork in this book was rendered digitally
The text is set in Cloister URW.

Edited by Jennifer Stokes
Designed by Michael Reis

Printed and bound in Malaysia, in 3/2018 by Tien Wah Press (Pte) Ltd.

CM 18 0 9 8 7 6 5 4 3 2 1

Library and Archives Canada Cataloguing in Publication

Fergus, Maureen, author
The reptile club / Maureen Fergus ; [illustrated by] Elina Ellis.

ISBN 978-1-77138-655-5 (hardcover)

I. Ellis, Elina, illustrator II. Title.

PS8611.E735R47 2018   jC813'.6   C2017-906645-5

The Reptile Club

Written by Maureen Fergus & Illustrated by Elina Ellis

Rory's FAVORITE THINGS:
- ☑ deep-fried pickles
- ☑ corduroy pants
- ☑ singing in the shower
- ☑ REPTILES!

Kids Can Press

There were lots of clubs at Rory's new school,
but none seemed quite right for him.

The Astronaut Club was
too intimidating.

The Prancing Unicorn Club was too frilly.

The Extra Math Homework Club wasn't nearly as much fun as Rory had thought it would be.

"Why don't you start your own club?" suggested his mom.

"Make it about something you love," advised his dad.

Rory loved deep-fried pickles, corduroy pants and singing in the shower.

But more than anything, Rory loved reptiles.

So the next day at school, Rory put up Reptile Club posters and handed out Reptile Club flyers.

No one seemed interested, but Rory didn't care. He just knew there were others out there who shared his passion for reptiles.

And he couldn't wait to meet them.

When the lunch bell rang on Friday, Rory set out his plastic reptile collection and the lizard-shaped lemon cookies his dad had helped him bake the night before.

Then he sat back and waited for his fellow reptile enthusiasts to arrive.

Rory waited ...   and waited ...   and waited.

Just when he was beginning to think that *no one* was going to
show up, he heard whispering in the hallway. Heart thumping,
he hurried over to see who it was.

For a long moment, Rory just stared at the crocodile, the anaconda and the gecko, and they just stared at him.

Then the crocodile cleared his throat and said, "Is this where the Reptile Club is meeting?"

"Yes," said Rory.

"Awesome!" said the crocodile. "My name is Raoul. I sweat through my mouth."

"My name is Miriam," said the anaconda. "I weigh 514 pounds and could swallow you in one bite."

"My name is Pierre," squeaked the gecko. "I have no eyelids, so I have to lick my eyeballs to keep them clean and moist."

"Nice to meet you all," said Rory. "My name is Rory. I sweat through my armpits, I can swallow a hotdog in one bite and I would give *anything* to be able to lick my eyeballs."

Everybody laughed.

Once the new club members were comfortably
settled, they talked about their favorite reptiles.

"My favorite reptile is my aunt Gladys because even though she tried to eat me shortly after I hatched, she always gets me terrific birthday presents," said Raoul.

"Carla Chameleon is my favorite reptile because she is the world's funniest practical joker," said Miriam.

"My favorite reptile is my friend Jamal because one time I accidentally ripped off his tail and he forgave me even before it grew back," said Pierre.

Next, the new club members shared interesting reptile facts.
"It is a fact that the grouchiest tortoise I ever met was 174 years old," said Raoul.

"It is a fact that I adore Rocky Rodent ice cream," sighed Miriam.

"It is a fact that I think Barry the basilisk lizard is a big show-off," sniffed Pierre.

Rory and his fellow club members spent the rest of the meeting playing and eating cookies. When the other kids returned from lunch and saw what the Reptile Club was all about, they couldn't wait to join.

At first, Raoul, Miriam and Pierre didn't want to let mammals into their club. Then Rory pointed out that *he* was a mammal, and also that it wasn't nice to be prejudiced against others just because they had hair and could regulate their body temperature.

After that, the reptiles agreed to welcome the mammals with open forelimbs.

In the weeks that followed, all sorts of strange and wonderful creatures joined the Reptile Club, and at every meeting they did something fun and different.

One week, they had a bake sale to raise money to buy a club pet.

The following week, they took a trip to the store to choose
their pet. The amphibians were all too slimy, the arachnids were
all too leggy and the insects were all too delicious-looking.
They settled on a cactus, which they named Cornelius.

They came up with a secret password and a secret hand signal.

They went on hikes to
observe the local wildlife.

They played games like
Hide and Shriek ...

and Guess What I Just Ate?

Never in the history of the world had
mammals and reptiles gotten along so well.

Then one blustery day in late autumn, Raoul said the words that Rory had been both dreading and expecting:

"It's time for us reptiles to go."

"Some of us will hibernate," said Miriam.

"The rest of us will head south," said Pierre.

"Why?" cried Rory's classmates.

"Because winter is coming and reptiles can't tolerate the cold," explained Rory.

Raoul shook Rory's hand and
promised that he'd never forget him.

Miriam hugged Rory tight and
told him that no mammal had ever
understood her so well.

Pierre licked Rory's right eyeball
and thanked him for everything.

One by one, the reptiles said goodbye forever.

That winter, not one of Rory's classmates quit the Reptile Club.
Partly this was because they'd become reptile enthusiasts, but
mostly it was because they'd become Rory's friends.

Rory appreciated their loyalty, but even he had to admit that without Raoul and the others, the Reptile Club meetings just weren't the same.

And that is why, one warm day in early spring, Rory had an idea.

"I think it's time for us to start a new club ..."

"The Dinosaur Club!"

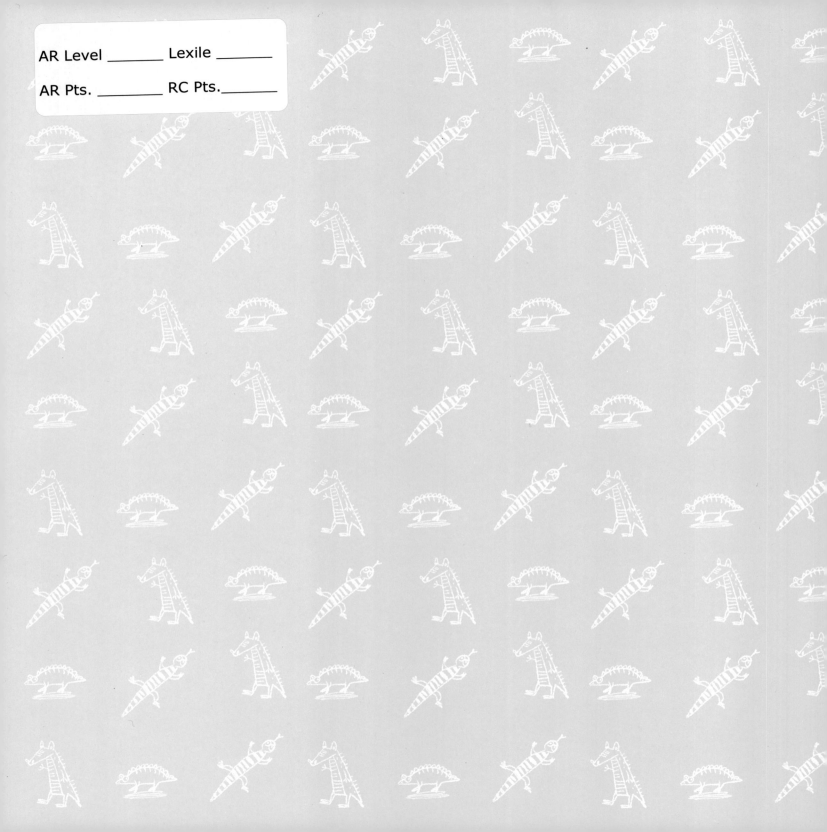

AR Level _____ Lexile _____

AR Pts. _____ RC Pts._____